First published in the United States of America in 2019 by Chronicle Books LLC.

Originally published in Catalan in 2017 under the title *Enigmas: Desafía Tu Mente Con 25 Historias de Misterio* by Zahorí Books in Barcelona, Spain.

Text copyright © 2017 by Ana Gallo.
Illustrations copyright © 2019 by Victor Escandell.
Translation copyright © 2019 by Chronicle Books LLC.
Library of Congress Cataloging-in-Publication Data available.

ISBN 978-1-4521-7713-7

Manufactured in China.

Original Zahorí Books edition design by Rebeka Elizegi and Victor Escandell.
Chronicle Books edition design by Lydia Ortiz.
English translation by Feather Flores.
Typeset in Diamond Girl.

10 9 8 7 6 5 4 3 2 1

Chronicle Books LLC
680 Second Street
San Francisco, California 94107

Chronicle Books—we see things differently.
Become part of our community at www.chroniclekids.com.

"Thank you Malena, Nico, Biel, Julia, Benat, and Naroa for always inspiring us, and for giving us ideas as fun as the ones in this book."
Victor + Rebeka

SLEUTH &SOLVE

20+ MIND-TWISTING MYSTERIES

by Victor Escandell

Adaptation of mysteries by Ana Gallo

chronicle books · san francisco

WELCOME TO
SLEUTH & SOLVE!

Get ready to solve mysteries that require two different ways of thinking and analyzing. Some are solved by using logic while others are solved with your imagination. The icons at the top of each mystery let you know how to proceed in each case.

 LOGIC    IMAGINATION

 USING LOGIC...

When you see the Logic icon, the mystery will present a setting and a clue.

- Read the whole case thoroughly and observe the illustrations carefully.
- Don't just offer the first solution that comes to mind. If you think you know the answer, check it by recreating the whole story with your solution in mind.
- Then ask yourself, *Do all of the elements make sense?*

> The solution lies in the text or in the illustrations. Read and observe carefully!

6

WE ALL THINK AND ANALYZE DIFFERENTLY!

Sleuthing successfully means changing your perspective and thinking creatively!

 USING IMAGINATION...

When you see the Imagination icon:

- These mysteries pose unusual situations and have surprising answers.
- Remember that although these mysteries appear to be simple, the logical answer is usually not the right one. You must use your imagination to solve them.
- Think outside the box. Approach the problem in a different way. For example, here is a brief puzzle and solution: My grandmother dropped an orange peel in her coffee cup, but it didn't get wet. Why not? (Answer: Because there were coffee grounds in her cup—not coffee!)

I figured it out!

7

HOW TO PLAY
SLEUTH & SOLVE!

You can solve these mysteries with family and friends. The more people participate, the more fun the game will be! But even if you are playing with just one other person, you will still enjoy the game. You can even play alone and solve the puzzles on your own. Then you will become a real detective, looking for clues and using both logic and imagination. There are a few ways to play:

AS A FAMILY

- Make sure you set aside enough time to play. You don't want to be rushed.
- For maximum fun, have several detectives participate (the more players, the more fun)!
- One person should look at the solution under the flap before you begin solving the mystery—they will be the Investigation Director (you can change the director for each case). The other detectives will ask questions about the case in order to get clues. The director can only respond with the following types of answers:
  - With a "yes" or "no."
  - By posing a question (when it's clear that some clue hasn't been understood).
  - With "It doesn't matter" (when the question isn't relevant to finding the solution).
- If you get stuck, the Investigation Director can help you review the clues and observe anything that may have been overlooked.

Give everyone time to talk and share the floor!

IN TEAMS

- Form teams of two or more detectives, and ask another person to act as a judge.
- Before you begin investigating, determine the number of cases each team will solve. To win, you don't have to solve the cases faster than other teams—you just have to earn more points!
- When a team finds the solution, tell the judge. The judge will determine whether the team has earned the points and may continue on to the next case.
- Every time a team solves a case, the judge will write down the points earned on a piece of paper. If there is a tie between teams, solve another case to resolve the tie.

To follow the points system, you can write down points on a sheet of paper or in a notebook.

REMEMBER, WE ALL THINK DIFFERENTLY! SOME CASES THAT MAY SEEM EASY TO YOU ARE DIFFICULT FOR OTHER PEOPLE, AND THE OTHER WAY AROUND.

AS A FAMILY

CASE	JUAN	ELISA	PEDRO	AMANDA
READING THE SIGNS	50			
THE STOLEN DOLL		30		
A CURIOUS ROBBERY			50	
CROSSING THE RIVER		50		
AN UNTIMELY RAIN				60
THE BOARDING SCHOOL				40
TWO DRINKS, PLEASE	50			
TOTAL POINTS	100	80	50	100

IN TEAMS

CASE	TEAM 1	TEAM 2
READING THE SIGNS	50	
THE STOLEN DOLL		
A CURIOUS ROBBERY		30
CROSSING THE RIVER		50
AN UNTIMELY RAIN	50	
THE BOARDING SCHOOL		60
TWO DRINKS, PLEASE	40	
	50	
TOTAL POINTS	190	140

BY YOURSELF
You can also solve these mysteries on your own and keep track of your points.

THE POINTS SYSTEM

The mysteries in this book are classified by difficulty level ranging from 1 to 6.
The levels are featured at the top of each page with stars:

1 = VERY EASY

★ ★ ★ ★ ★ ★

6 = VERY DIFFICULT

★ ★ ★ ★ ★ ★

In addition, each difficulty level has a different point value.

LEVEL	POINTS
★ ★ ★ ★ ★ ★	10
★ ★ ★ ★ ★ ★	20
★ ★ ★ ★ ★ ★	30
★ ★ ★ ★ ★ ★	40
★ ★ ★ ★ ★ ★	50
★ ★ ★ ★ ★ ★	60

TABLE OF CONTENTS

Look carefully at the icons to figure out whether you should apply logic or use your imagination.

11

A LIGHT GUILT

click!

Marco lives and works in his home by the sea where he has lived alone for many years. His life is very routine, and each night before going to bed he turns on the light.

1 But one night, Marco is so tired that he forgets to turn on the light.

2 When he wakes up in the morning, he hears terrible news.

3 Marco is distraught, and then runs straight to the police to confess his guilt.

Officer, I am guilty!

WHY IS MARCO AT FAULT?

THE PRINCIPAL DETECTIVE

OUT OF ORDER

It's the beginning of summer and the school's office air-conditioning isn't working. Suddenly, the secretary realizes that somebody has stolen the thumb drive from her computer containing all of the end-of-year exam questions. The school's principal asks everyone who was near the computer around the time of the disappearance what they were doing.

14

1 "I was on the phone helping several people," the secretary replies.

2 "I was leaning on the table, writing down some notes," the deliveryman says.

3 "I was going to ask the secretary if she'd seen my sweater," the accountant explains.

Principal

4 "I came to make some photocopies," the student says.

WHO TOOK THE THUMB DRIVE?

15

THIEF ON BOARD

A Japanese fishing boat sets off to work on the high seas.
At the end of the day, the captain decides to take a shower
and leaves his valuable gold watch on the table in his cabin.

1 But when he gets out of the shower, his watch is gone! To find the thief, he asks each crew member what they were doing while he was in the shower.

2 The cook says that he was making dinner in the kitchen.

3 The mechanic says that she was in the machine room checking the generator.

4 The ship's officer says that she was in her cabin taking a nap.

Ugh, that was some dream!

5 The watchman explains that the boat's flag was upside down, so he was on the deck fixing it.

WHO IS LYING?

17

ALL BOTTLED UP

Katia's grandfather was obsessed with magic. When he died, he left her a glass bottle with
a key inside, but it was stopped with a cork. On the bottle was a note:
"If you can retrieve this key without removing the cork or breaking the bottle,
your mother will give you the box that it opens."

1 Katia stares at the bottle all day, trying to think of a solution.

2 She asks her brother to help, but he can't think of a way to get the key, either.

3 Katia rereads the note:

...WITHOUT REMOVING THE CORK OR BREAKING THE BOTTLE...

4 Suddenly, Katia's face lights up: She knows what to do!

Eureka! I've got it!

HOW DOES KATIA GET THE KEY?

19

THE SILENT WITNESS

Martina rests peacefully in the bedroom on the top floor. Her eyes are open as she begins to drift into sleep. Everything is calm, with the only sound coming from the television downstairs.

SUDDENLY, THE DOOR OPENS AND THREE THIEVES ENTER THE BEDROOM.

1 Martina looks straight at the thieves.

2 Martina listens to the thieves' hurried movements without ever moving herself.

3 The thieves take everything!

4 When they finally leave, Martina is asleep and doesn't notify the police.

WHY DOES MARTINA STAY SO QUIET? ?

21

READING THE SIGNS

From her upstairs window, Rita peers at the new neighbors
across the street who moved in just a few days ago. It is nighttime
when she witnesses something very strange . . .

1 Rita sees the husband watching television peacefully.

2 She also spies his wife sitting next to him, reading a book.

3 After a few minutes, the man gets up and turns off all the lights before leaving the room.

4 But the woman stays in the dark and continues to read her book quietly.

HOW IS THE WOMAN STILL READING WITHOUT THE LIGHTS ON?

THE STOLEN DOLL

24

A valuable Russian nesting doll has disappeared from an antiques store. It once belonged to an ancestor of a Russian tsar and is very valuable (but only the store owner knows this). The new saleswoman, Andrea, had just been put in charge of the display case when the doll disappeared. Without informing any of his employees of the doll's value, the store owner speaks with everyone to find out who may have stolen the doll.

1 Mark, the manager, suspects the new saleswoman, Andrea, because…

Until she arrived, nothing had ever gone missing.

2 Andrea assures her boss that …

I would never do anything to endanger my new job.

3 Tati, the cashier, says that …

I didn't even know the old doll was so valuable.

4 After speaking with his employees, the store owner knows who stole the doll.

HOW DOES HE KNOW WHO THE THIEF IS?

25

A CURIOUS ROBBERY

The police inspector doesn't know what to think. Alex arrives at the police station with a very strange complaint: He says that after he left his parked car to get coffee, his house was stolen.

26

1 The inspector is confused and asks Alex to clarify the details of the theft.

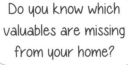

Do you know which valuables are missing from your home?

2 Alex says that he doesn't know.

I don't know, Inspector.

3 "So how do you know that you've been robbed?" the inspector asks. Alex responds: "Because when I came back from drinking my coffee, my house wasn't there anymore!"

THE INSPECTOR IS CONFUSED...

WHAT REALLY HAPPENED?

CROSSING THE RIVER

To get home to his farm from the market, a man must always cross the river in his little boat. One day, he and his faithful dog return from the market where he has bought a chicken and a sack of corn.

THIS BOAT IS VERY SMALL AND CAN ONLY FIT ME AND ONE OTHER OBJECT.

HOW CAN I GET EVERYTHING HOME?

1 If he crosses with the dog, the chicken will eat the corn.

 →

2 If he crosses with the corn, the dog will eat the chicken.

 ←

HOW SHOULD HE CROSS THE RIVER? ?

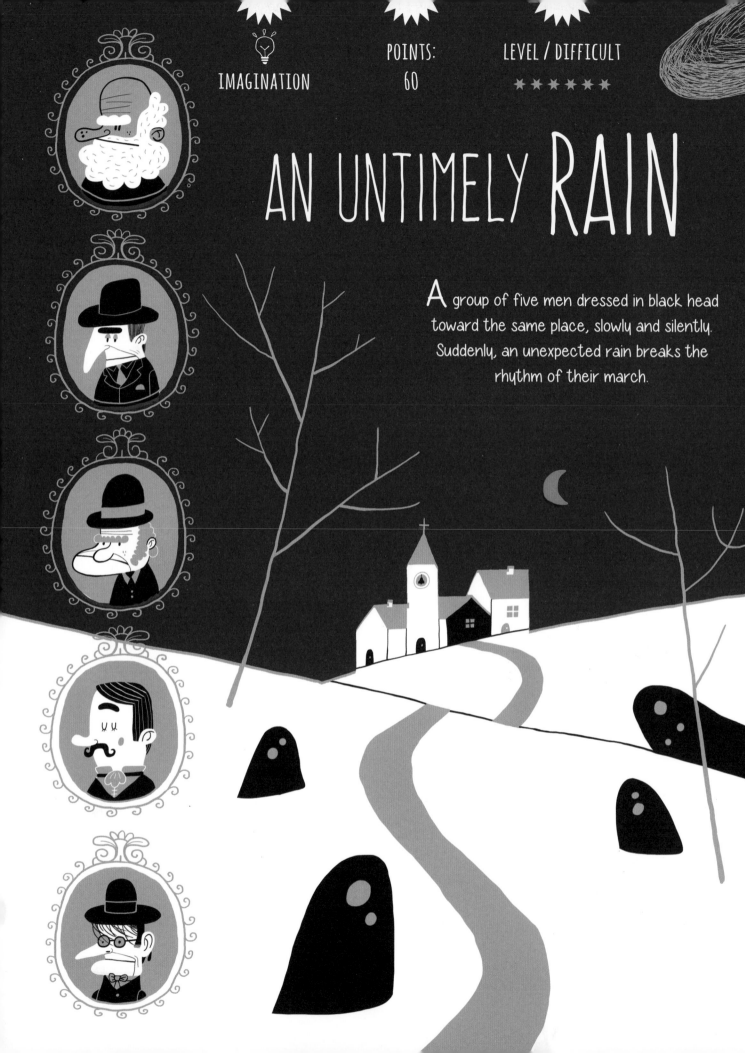

AN UNTIMELY RAIN

A group of five men dressed in black head toward the same place, slowly and silently. Suddenly, an unexpected rain breaks the rhythm of their march.

1 The five men leave the village and move together in the direction of the cemetery.

2 When it starts to rain, four of the men accelerate their pace, but the fifth man does not.

3 The four men who sped up arrive at their destination completely soaked, but the fifth man remains dry.

WHY DID FOUR OF THE MEN GET WET, BUT NOT THE FIFTH?

POINTS:
40

LEVEL / MEDIUM
★★★★★★

THE BOARDING SCHOOL

The boarding school is quiet and peaceful on this Sunday as summer begins. There are only a few students still around, and the only staff remaining are the cook and one teacher.

32

1 The cook prepares Sunday lunch.

2 The teacher stops grading the final essays in order to eat lunch.

3 Alice says she's going to see if the mail has arrived.

4 Clara is lying on her bed listening to her favorite music.

RRRRIIINGG!

SUDDENLY, THE TEACHER PULLS THE FIRE ALARM, SHOUTING, "SOMEONE BURNED THE ESSAYS WHILE I WAS EATING!"

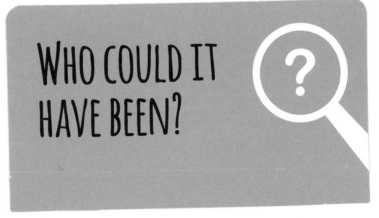

WHO COULD IT HAVE BEEN? ?

TWO DRINKS, PLEASE

Luca and Antonio are two dangerous mobsters with a long list of enemies who would like to kill them. One night, they go to a restaurant where they eye the other patrons suspiciously. After all, they never know where danger might be lurking . . .

34

1 Both men ask for a soda. The waiter carefully prepares the drinks, which are served with lots of ice.

2 Luca is thirsty and finishes his drink in seconds.

3 By contrast, Antonio slowly savors his drink while stirring the ice with his straw.

WHEN THEY GET UP FROM THE TABLE, ANTONIO IMMEDIATELY COLLAPSES.

WHAT HAPPENED TO ANTONIO?

THE IMPOSSIBLE PRISON

Escape...

Escape...

Escape...

Escape...

Three prisoners share the same cell and motivation: They want to escape! But in order to break out of prison, they must overcome one big inconvenience . . .

36

1 The window of the cell is so high that it doesn't even have bars, since it's impossible to reach.

2 First, the prisoners get on a bunk and try to stand on each other's shoulders, but they can't reach the window.

3 Then, they decide to dig a tunnel. When they realize that it's going to take too long, they give up.

4 Suddenly, one of the prisoners realizes that there is one way to reach the window and escape!

HOW DO THEY GET TO THE WINDOW? ?

THE SENTENCE

In the legendary kingdom of Babar Khan, the punishment for stealing is death. One day, a clueless visitor who doesn't know about this law is caught stealing fruit from the palace gardens.

38

THE KING LETS THE THIEF CHOOSE WHICH OF THESE FOUR CELLS HE WANTS TO DIE IN, INFORMING HIM THAT IF HE CHOOSES WELL, HE MIGHT BE SAVED . . .

1 The cell of eternal fire, which is engulfed in flames as soon as the prisoner comes through the door.

BURN, BURN...

2 The cell of beasts, where starving tigers, each deprived of food for a year, await the prisoner.

3 The cell of swords, a dungeon where the most ruthless guards take bets on who will kill their victims in the most gruesome way.

4 The cell of the dragon, where the prisoner will confront a three-headed dragon and its three poisonous tongues.

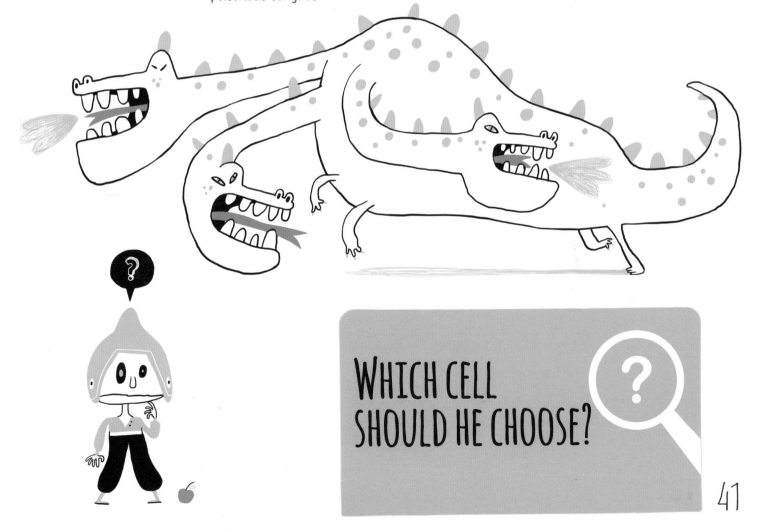

WHICH CELL SHOULD HE CHOOSE? ?

THE SULTAN'S SUCCESSOR

Centuries ago, in a kingdom far, far away, there lived an aging sultan who wanted to name one of his two sons the successor to the throne before his death. To determine the successor, he gave them a somewhat strange test: Both of the men were to ride through the desert until they reached the oasis, but the son whose horse came in last place would be declared the sultan's successor.

42

THE TWO SONS RODE THROUGH THE DESERT TOWARD THE OASIS,
BUT EACH STOPPED TO THINK BEFORE REACHING IT.

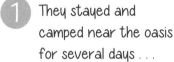

1 They stayed and camped near the oasis for several days . . .

2 . . . and for several nights, each thinking about how they could possibly win the throne.

3 Suddenly, a wise man passing by gave them the solution, uttering only three words.

4 Both sons did what the wise man proposed, each spurring the horses to arrive at the oasis first.

WHAT DID THE WISE MAN TELL THEM? ?

A STRANGER IN THE FIELD

One wet spring day, a farmer is walking through his fields. It is rare for anyone to approach the valley where his farm lies, since it is isolated among the mountains and far from any towns or cities. The only sound is of birds chirping. However, on this particular morning . . .

44

1 The farmer finds a man lying on his back under a large tree. The stranger is stunned and has a wounded leg.

2 There is no trace of footprints or tire tracks on the wet earth.

3 The farmer sees that the man is wearing a backpack.

HOW DID THE MAN GET HERE? ?

SURPRISE ATTACK

Everyone sleeps peacefully in the village, confident that the army will protect them from being attacked by intruders. Each night, a soldier stands guard and watches the edges of the forest surrounding the village.

1 During his shift, the sleeping guard dreams that intruders attack the village.

2 When he awakes, the soldier tells the Captain of the Guard about his dream, and the Captain doubles the village's reinforcements.

3 The intruders attack that night, but the village is not taken by surprise.

4 However, the Captain arrests the soldier who warned him of the attack.

You're arrested!

WHY WAS THE SOLDIER ARRESTED?

47

WRONG WAY

After stealing a car, a thief decides to go to the mall in search of unsuspecting shoppers whose wallets he can steal.

SHOPPING

48

1. To get to the mall without being seen, the thief takes a very narrow street.

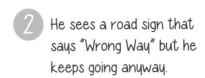

2. He sees a road sign that says "Wrong Way" but he keeps going anyway.

3. At the end of the street, the thief encounters a police officer directing traffic.

4. The police officer doesn't stop or fine him. She lets him continue on his way.

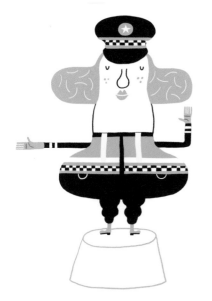

WHY DOESN'T THE POLICE OFFICER ARREST THE THIEF?

49

ALL WAS CALM

It's a rainy Saturday morning, and all is calm and cozy in the Johnson family mansion. Like every weekend, everyone sleeps in, eats breakfast together, and then enjoys their favorite activities.

1 Little Pat is having fun chasing the cat.

2 Mr. Johnson is reading the news on his computer.

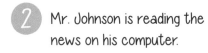

3 Mary is listening to music in her room.

4 Mrs. Johnson is completely engrossed in her book.

5 Edgar, the gardener, is watering the flowers in the garden like he does every Saturday.

6 Suddenly, everyone hears a scream from Mr. Johnson's office. When they enter the room, they discover his corpse on the ground.

WHO IS THE MURDERER?

A FORTUNATE FALL

Two window cleaners have come to clean the windows of a 50-story building. Although they have a strong scaffolding platform to keep them from falling, they suffer an unexpected accident while working.

1 Lucas and Marian step onto the scaffolding platform to start cleaning the windows.

2 A pulley lifts the scaffold so the cleaners can start working.

3 Suddenly, a light breeze becomes a forceful wind, violently shaking the scaffold.

AH!

WHOOOOOOSh!

4 Lucas and Marian swing off the scaffold and fall to the ground, but they both survive!

HOW DID THEY SURVIVE THE FALL? ?

A CODE FOR DETECTIVES

Mr. Green has been found dead at his desk during the party that he was hosting in his very own magnificent house! There are no signs of violence, but upon close examination, a red note is discovered clutched in his left hand. This strange note, which is written in code, is the key to finding the culprit.

55

Inspector Lewis is called in to investigate.
He looks for clues that may be hiding in plain sight.

THE LIST OF SUSPECTS IS VERY LONG . . .

1 Emilia is Mr. Green's oldest employee.

2 Sebastian is Mr. Green's son, and the pianist hired for entertainment at the party.

3 Donna is Sebastian's girlfriend.

4 Mr. Quincy is Mr. Green's neighbor and the owner of a nearby mansion.

5 Simon is Mr. Green's cousin. He has a gold pocket watch.

6 Professor Nassar is a scholar of Roman law who bores everyone at parties.

7 Eric is an old friend of Mr. Green's who often spends weekends at the house.

8 Lady Adolfina is a close friend of Mr. Green's and a regular at his parties.

9 Dr. Adams has been Mr. Green's doctor for many years.

10 Brenda is Eric's friend, and she always accompanies him on his travels.

What do these mysterious dates mean?

CAN THE SOLUTION BE FOUND IN THIS NOTE!

2ND FEBRUARY,
3RD MARCH,
4TH APRIL,
2ND OCTOBER

WHO IS THE MURDERER?

GOING UP

Mr. Curt of apartment 7A likes rainy days much more than sunny days. When it rains, he takes advantage of the weather and runs his errands, takes out the trash, goes to the movies, and is out and about all day. On rainy days, his life becomes much more comfortable . . .

SUNNY DAYS

5TH FLOOR

1 On sunny days, Mr. Curt only takes the elevator to the fifth floor. From there he proceeds to the seventh floor on foot, taking the stairs for the last two floors. By the time he arrives home, he is very tired and grumpy!

HUFF
HUFF
Huff

RAINY DAYS

2 By contrast, Mr. Curt goes directly up to the seventh floor on rainy days.

7TH FLOOR

WHY DOES MR. CURT ONLY TAKE THE ELEVATOR TO THE FIFTH FLOOR ON SUNNY DAYS, WHEN ON RAINY DAYS HE GOES DIRECTLY TO THE SEVENTH FLOOR?

WHY DO MR. CURT'S HABITS CHANGE WITH THE WEATHER? ?

59

THE SERVER'S SURPRISE

HICCUP!

TAPAS

TAPAS

One hot summer morning, a man enters a restaurant, looking for something to drink that will quench his thirst. He has no idea what an unusual surprise awaits him inside . . .

1 The man opens the door and enters the restaurant.

HICCUP!

2 He approaches the bar and asks a server for a cold lemonade.

HICCUP!

3 Suddenly, the server makes the scariest face the man has ever seen!

4 After a while, the man leaves the restaurant and thanks the server effusively.

AAHHHHH!

THANK YOU SO MUCH!

WHY IS THE MAN GRATEFUL?